COMMITTED

Olivia's Sixth Wish

Daphne Dennis

Copyright

Social Stamina – 1,2,3 Let's Go!

Titles to help look at things from other perspectives and strengthen your mindset.

The Great Ascension–1,2,3 Let's Go!

Titles to help you gain focus and climb the ladder of success!

How to Start – 1,2,3 Let's Go!

Titles to help you with step-by-step, must-have knowledge of the business world and personal experiences.

Top 10 Questions to Ask Before You…1,2,3 Let's Go!

Titles with must-have questions (and logic behind) for many of life's daily and major decisions.

Find our fiction below!

https://www.ttpublishinghouse.com/legendsreborn

https://www.ttpublishinghouse.com/7wishes

https://www.ttpublishinghouse.com/mallcadet

Social Media

Facebook: tlmpublishinghouse

Website: www.TTpublishinghouse.com

Want to Read for Free?

You may qualify for a spot on our Advance Reader Copy group.

Never heard of an ARC Group?

Simply put, it's a small group of people who are interested in a specific genre and are invited to read books before they're published.

Your feedback can help alter the storyline or even catch an elusive typo!

You're asked to provide an honest review when it is published, and that's it!

You read for free!

Go now to confirm your interest in the ARC Group!
https://www.ttpublishinghouse.com/joinTLMarc

CONTENTS

UNFAMILIAR TERRITORY

Twelve hours later, and Cade's words are still ringing in my head. I can hear them; the words, the way he said it, his beautiful voice, if I close my eyes and really concentrate, I can still hear them. It is a joy to relive that moment over and over again, and it is also a problem, because even as I revel in it, I remember it is tainted with my bad decision. What was I thinking?! That girl that almost gave a total stranger- I can't even say it- you-know-what. After everything that happened with me and Cade in the sporting store; the sweet moments we had, the joy I shared with Cade when he got the news about Kayla, and the sweet moments we shared after, the next day, I guess I just felt closer to him than I had felt all through the trip, and seeing him letting loose, and being so free with Nat and Elena, it gave the impression that maybe I was alone in my feelings. Fear. That was what I felt, it was the catalyst of all things stupid I did yesterday.

But, today is a new day, and I'm determined to make the most of it. Cade professed his feelings for me. That had to mean something. I know, I know, it wasn't done based on purely his decision, my wish had a lot to do with it. But then again, my wish clearly stated that 'if Cade was the one for me', so if we weren't meant to end up together, it wouldn't even have worked, Cade would not have professed anything. So, in a roundabout way, I guess my wish was only just a nudge in what would have happened on its own anyway. Ah, who am I kidding? I feel terrible. Feelings shouldn't be nudged, they are either felt, or they are not. Man, this was so not worth it.

Still ruminating on that, I hear a knock on my door. That must be Cade. After the bonfire last night, I and Cade had driven to a hotel a few miles away, and we had booked adjoining rooms. Nat and Elena had tried to convince us to stay with them in their rented cabin on the beach, but Cade had declined and honestly, that had been fine by me. I had had enough of dangerous Latinas and booze filled environments that just begged for bad decisions.

Today is for exploration, of the California Coastline. Finally.

"Olivia?", Cade's voice comes through my door.

"Yeah", I reply. I try to tame my wild hair by pulling it into a loose ponytail, few wayward strands fall out anyway. I hop to the door, and open it.

Seeing all six feet of Care standing on the other side, and watching his silver eyes darken just slightly as they take me in, steadily and slowly, from head to toe, brought on the awareness that I was wearing only a very thin tank top and boxer shorts.

My face heats up, or at least that's what it feels like as I feel the heat in my cheeks. I shift on my feet, suddenly uncomfortable. God, I hate this. Where did the comfortable feeling I shared with Cade go to? Where did the absolute sense of peace I always felt when I was with him disappear to? They are now buried in the aftermath of a stupid decision, that's where. Now I feel all awkward and embarrassed.

Make smart decisions, kids.

Cade clears his throat, and kind of looked through me. He didn't look over my head like he could have, easily, but he also didn't look me in the eye either.

"Um, are you ready?", he asks.

I automatically look down at myself, he does too. Our eyes come up at the same time.

"No, I guess not", he says, and I think I detect a slight hint of humor in his eyes, but I don't know. I had become quite good at reading Cade's eyes, and the emotions in them, but after yesterday, I feel like he is now a stranger, all over again.

"Hey, I'll be downstairs, in the lobby. When you're done, come meet me there, sounds good?"

I nod my head. "Yeah, sounds good."

He nods too, and then, still not looking directly at me, he backs away from the door, and walk away.

I close the door, and lean against it, I sigh. Shit.

***

A half hour later, I head out of my room, down to the lobby. I am now wearing a yellow off-shoulder flowery summer dress top, and fitted jeans that goes tucked down into a pair of one of my favorite boots, my hair is let down and it flows down to my back, a brown cowgirl hat rests lightly on top of it. Yes, I am the epitome of sunshine, and it is intentional. I will have fun today if it kills me, and this awkwardness between I and Cade will have to be resolved.

This whole situation makes me realize just how important Cade has come to be in my life, and I will not let a petty thing like this come between us. I stop at the entrance of the lobby, scanning the large room for Cade's familiar frame. My eyes come to rest on him, he is seated in one of the lounge chairs, on the edge of it, and he wrings his hands nervously. I sigh. This is because of me, I know it, it's because of the way things were between us when he came up to my room to call me. This ends now, I have to clear this shit up.

I take a deep breath, and walk towards me. He doesn't feel me until I am a couple feet away from me, and then suddenly, he brings up his head, and meets my eyes. Our eyes lock, and I feel a familiar rush of feeling course through me, and I recognize it as the *zing* that is common to I and Cade, when we first met. That charged electricity that flooded us both on that very first day, when we hadn't even known each other's names, when we hadn't even known what we were going to mean to one another. I feel it again, and suddenly, just like that, I know everything is going to be alright.

Strangely, I feel my eyes watering, but I blink them back, now is not the time for tears, it is the time to set things right. I clear my throat, and take a step towards Cade. But as I am about to speak, Cade stands up from the chair, and comes to stand in front of me, directly, looking right at me. This time, not through me, not above me, right at me. He looks down, into my eyes, my eyes meet his, and my breath is knocked out of me at the intense gaze in his eyes. In the space of the moment, I see a lot go through Cade's silver-grey eyes, they hit me almost all at once, and because of the briefness of each one, I can't make out what they are, but one remains constant through it all; possessiveness. The raw, undiluted energy of it shines clear through to me from Cade's eyes. It's as if his eyes keep saying, no, shouting; *you're mine.* And the man behind the eyes is not trying to hide it, he's telling me.

I stare right back into his eyes, and will mine to let him know I agree. I am his. I know this as surely as I feel his rough coarse big hands gently frame my face.

In a quiet voice meant only for me, like more than a hundred people weren't milling about the lobby space, Cade says, "I am sorry for the position I put you in yesterday. I am not sorry for the words", he pauses here, our eyes still locked, and then he continues, "because I meant every word."

My heart does a wonderfully painful gallop at his words. I fight to keep my eyes steady on him as he continues.

"I am not sorry about the words, but I understand how uncomfortable you might feel by them, because me saying them changes the dynamics of our relationship, and it may be a change that you are not quite ready for yet. I understand that, and I am sorry for doing that to you."

A lump has now formed in my throat, I swallow deeply. Cade is still holding my face in his hands like we are the only two people in the world, and I realize I do not mind it at all. I could stay in the invincible bubble we create ourselves forever, and I would not care. I would die a happy, content, woman.

I say my words slowly, because I want him to be sure without a doubt about what I want to say next. "I am not uncomfortable. I am ready and happy about the change to the dynamics of our relationship. I want this. I want you."

I watch as Cade's eyes darken at my words. At this very moment, if anyone asks me what my favorite thing about Cade was, I would say his eyes, because as I watch them darken, I know they are showing an emotion far stronger and clearer than any word he could ever say with his mouth. And the feeling of knowing exactly what they mean, and the knowledge of knowing that I caused that reaction in him, fills with such power, a heady power I never knew I had. Confirming I have the same feelings for him as he does for me is important to him, and I can see just how important, in his eyes.

I frame his face too, and regret washes over me. "I am so sorry for being that person that I was yesterday. I hate that I did that, I hate that I made us feel that awkwardness because of my reckless act", I say, apology heavy in my voice.

"Don't apologize. That's in the past, and I think I have an idea why you did it. I was insensitive to you, and your feelings, I left you feeling doubtful, and I am sorry for that", Cade says. I smile. "Besides", a playful look comes into his eyes, "it was sexy" he says, grinning.

"What?!" I swat his arm playfully. "It's not funny, why are you grinning?"

He full-on laughs now. "Are you sure? It is pretty funny."

I step back from him, or at least, I try to, Cade holds on firmly to me, his eyes still laughing. I try to act offended. "Well, if it's so funny, you can laugh all you want, by yourself. I'm leaving."

I turn to leave, but Cade draws me back, hugging me to his chest. I can't help it, I inhale him.

Beneath my fingers, his chest rumbles with silent laughter, the purely male movement does something to my insides. My lower belly tightens, and I feel a pulsing between my legs. While I am still trying to process that lustful reaction to Cade's chest, he leans down, and whispers in my ear, "Yesterday, I couldn't laugh if my life depended on it. It was too fucking sexy."

Oh my God

The pulsing morphs into thrumming, I feel hot all over, and suddenly my fingertips- which are still on Cade's chest- grow hot, like they are on fire. I remain the way I am, face buried to his chest. I couldn't move if my life depended on it. And it just might.

Still reeling, Cade suddenly draws back, and draws on my hand, "Come on", he says.

"What? Where?", I ask, stupefied.

Still walking towards the entrance, and pulling me with him, Cade spares a glance back at me, "To be us again."

MUIR WOODS

Cade push open the doors, and we step outside to the cool summer breeze. People are milling about, different people in their idea of summer cloths.

Cade brings out his phone, and looks down at it, he frowns slightly.

"What's wrong?", I ask.

He lifts his head, and looks at me. "It's just, uh, this agenda I made for today, I wrote it out this morning actually. I searched online through places we could visit, things we could do, while we were here, and I compiled a list based on them."

I nod slowly, not seeing the problem. "Okay, so what's the problem?"

Cade shifts on his feet, a sure sign he is uncomfortable, he runs a hand through his hair. "Well, the thing is, I arranged the list in a way that would help- or, at least, would have helped- our situation this morning." I cock my head to the side, still confused. "What I mean is, this morning, because we still had that weird awkwardness between us, I planned our day to start with a walk, through Muir woods, just beyond the city."

My eyebrows come up. "Muir woods?"

Cade scratches a spot behind his ear, looking so uncomfortable I just want to hug him tight. "Yeah. Stupid, I know, but I just thought a walk through the woods would have a calming effect on us, and give us the privacy we need, or, needed, to talk", he says, and looks at me again. "But now that we have sorted the issue, sort of, it just feels…. boring, now, I guess."

I smile, totally besotted by Cade's adorable uneasiness. He turns off his phone, and pockets it. "You know what? Screw that, screw the walk in the woods, let's go to Venice Beach."

He turns to start walking, I put a hand on his arm to stop him. "Why don't you let me talk too, uh?" Cade turns back fully to me. "I think the walk sounds nice", Cade's eyebrows come up, I nod, "Yeah, I really do. And frankly, you thinking I wouldn't enjoy a walk just tells me you don't know me at all", I say, suddenly feeling dejected.

"Oh, I know you. I know a day indoors, curled up with a book, would be a perfect day, for you." I smile. "But I also know, because you are a homebody, - and I mean that in the best way possible- it would make you appreciate the outdoors that much more. And so, when you go on those rare outdoor trips, you would want to make the best of it, and do the craziest thing you can think of."

His words touch something deep in me. "You do know me", I say, smiling through the sudden sting of tears in my eyes.

Cade smiles back. "I do."

"Well, you are correct, about everything. But, concerning the walk, there is one variable you failed to account for, a variable that happens to be very important", I pause, Cade is confused, I smile up at him, "You", I say.

"Me?"

I nod, "Hmm, you. I want to walk through the woods with you. We have the rest of the day to do the craziest shit we can think of, but before any of that, I want to walk with you. Just you and me."

And just like that, I am lost in Cade's eyes, we are on the pavement just outside the hotel, people are milling past, and we stand, staring into each other's eyes like we're the only ones there. All I can think is; this is the greatest feeling ever.

As if he can sense what I'm thinking, Cade smiles, "Then let's walk", he says.

Minutes later, we get to Muir woods, tall trees stretch farther than I would have ever thought possible for a tree, I look up, squinting my face, trying to see their end. Beside me, Cade chuckles, "Don't even try", he says.

"Wow", I say, marveling at the woods stretched out before us. I close my eyes, and inhale deeply, the scent of fresh leaves and dewy grass assail my lungs. "This should be an everyday scene", I say, looking around in wonder at the bright greenery environment of the woods.

Cade takes my hand, and we start walking into the woods. I look down at our linked hands, and I feel a thrill run through my arm at the contact, I look up, and find myself staring into Cade's eyes. A warmth spreads through me at the tenderness I see there.

"It can be an everyday scene, if we bother to take caring for the environment seriously", Cade says, in response to my earlier comment.

I do a double take, smiling up at Cade. He looks down at me, and sees my expression of mild surprise. "What?", he asks.

Still smiling, I reply, "Nothing. I just didn't know you were so passionate about the environment."

Cade smiles too. "I am, as should the rest of the world be", he says.

"That is a nice thing to know about you, Cade Vulcan", I say, smiling at him. We pass over broken branches, the earth wet and soft beneath our feet as we walk, our hands are still linked. Walking like this with Cade, I definitely didn't envision this when I started out on my trip. It had been meant to be a self-developing trip, a time for me and my thoughts, and now, even though that is not exactly what I am doing, I am bettering myself, I feel I am. Being with Cade has been nothing but positive, he has shown me sides of life I hadn't seen before, and that I don't think I would have ever been able to see, without him. This trip is better than anything I could have ever thought of, because of Cade. I look up at him, at his face, a face that I now know as I well as my own, I know the face he makes when he is happy, sad, uncomfortable, I know he shifts on his feet when he is nervous, and that he scratches the tip of his ear and furrows his brows when he is confused, I know that his accent comes through when he is in an intense moment, - like he usually is with me when we get locked in each other's eyes- and I know he has the biggest heart of anyone I have ever come across.

I know him, and yet I feel crazy for it. This is not normal, two complete strangers can't just meet, - the meeting being courtesy of a magical wish, nonetheless- spend less than a week with each other, and feel this strongly about each other. Crazy is an understatement. And yet, slowly, I am heading off into real and deep emotional feelings anytime I look at Cade.

My troubling thoughts must have somehow projected themselves outwardly, because Cade stops walking, and turns to face me. He frames my face, and he does it oh so gently that I close my eyes for a second, I lean into the warmth and tenderness of his hand, and let myself feel.

"Hey, what's wrong?", Cade asks, concern heavy in his tone.

I open my eyes, and look into his. I'm sure my worry is clear enough in them as I ask, "Are we crazy?"

Cade's eyes crinkle in a smile, he nods his head, "Yeah, we definitely are."

I smile too, but shake my head, "I'm serious, Cade, people just don't have these feelings that we have, for each other. Definitely not within a short period of time like we do."

"No, they don't, because this is all us. This, these feelings that we feel for each other, this is all us, Olivia. Just you and me, right here, right now, okay?"

I look into his eyes, the silver in them seem to darken even more under the canopy of the trees around us, but I see his sincerity shine through, loud and clear. I smile, and nod.

"Good", Cade says, he links his fingers though mine again, "We're going to Venice Beach."

ART AND CULTURE

Venice Beach is chaotic, bright colors fly high and proud, and it is like everywhere I look, someone is laughing loudly or playing a ridiculous game. The streets are packed to an almost choking level, with tourist shops, restaurants, boutiques, all arranged one after the other in no particular order. As we walk past, a group of teenagers walk by, all of them dressed in brightly colored summer cloths, they make excited noises as they walk past. A blonde teenage girl among them lets out a high whistle, and it just happens to coincide with the exact time I walk past her, I swear the whistle goes straight to my head. I cover my ear with my hand, pausing momentarily to look back at the group, the blonde does not even realize she almost made someone deaf, because she just continues making whistle noises and catcalls with the rest of her group as they bounce on happily.

My hand still on my ear, I look back at Cade, to find him grinning. My eyebrow comes up, "Is something funny?", I ask.

Cade chuckles, "Oh come on, surely you remember how it was to be that young and free", he says.

"Right now, I can barely hear birds sing!", I exclaim, pointing to my still ringing ear.

Cade throws back his head, and laughs. He throws his hand around my shoulders, and starts walking again, I pretend to resist, but then I tag along, smiling.

We arrive in front of a craft shop, I look around at the hand-woven beads, molded African sculptures, and paper-mâché art.

"Wow, these are beautiful", I say.

An average-built woman comes out of the inner portion of the shop. She smiles as she sees us, and her white teeth shine, all the more brightly because of her dark shiny skin. "Hello, welcome! You look so beautiful", she says, looking at me, her eyes smiling at me.

Because her flawless skin and beautiful face structure- a combination that flat-out intimidates me- focuses on me as she says this, I fluster, staggered by the compliment. "Oh, um, thanks", I say, "But, I mean, you're the beautiful one", I return the compliment.

She smiles, and dimples flash, "Thank you", she replies, "You are free to roam around, and pick anything that catches your fancy, just holler at me if you need anything. My name is Mojisola, but you can call me Mo."

I nod, "Thanks."

She smiles at me, and then at Cade. New customers wander in, and she starts to make her way towards them, but Cade stops her with a question.

"What part of Africa is your shop themed around?"

"Nigeria. I have varieties of diverse African cultures, but I'm from Nigeria, the Yoruba tribe, specifically, so I mostly have items from that part", Mo replies to Cade's question.

Cade nods. "Nice. Thanks."

Mo smiles. "You're welcome. Just let me know if you need anything", she says again, and with her bright smile effortlessly still in place, turns to her new customers.

I look around the shop, at the impressive collection. "So, what do we get?", I ask Cade.

He looks around too, "Everything in here will have a story, every bead, every sculpture, every one of them will have a traditional story attached to it, that's how most African cultures work. We just have to find something that speaks to us."

I nod, looking around me, my eyes come to land on a set of tiny beads, they are of different colors and are arranged in a row that's too wide to be a bracelet, eight of these rows are arranged on top of one another. I draw on Cade's arm, calling his attention, I point at it. "What do you think these are?"

Cade leans down to look at the beads with me, his brows furrow. "I don't know", he says after a while. We both look around the shop, trying to find Mo, our eyes lock on her at the same time as hers lock on ours. As if she could sense we had questions, she walks over to us.

"What's up?", Mo asks.

"We just wanted to know what these", Cade points to the rows of beads, "are, you know, what they mean to your culture, the Nigerian culture."

Mo smiles her brilliant smile again, "It's very intuitive of you to know that they have a meaning to them. Well, so basically the story behind them is that they are objects of decoration, you know, but not just any kind of decoration. You can't wear them around your neck, or your wrists, or anything like that, and even though both genders wear most beads as decorative objects all the time, these particular sets of beads are meant for the women, and they wear it around their waist."

"Woah, their waist?", I ask.

"Yep. Majority of Nigerian men find it very attractive. First of all, they are around a very seductive part of the body, I mean, the waist? The waist is a very sexy part of the body. I'm sure Cade agrees", Mo says, turning to Cade with a smile.

"Uh….", he thinks about it for a while, like a second, really, and then he grins, "oh, yeah, yeah, definitely sexy", he says, grinning so wide, "I had a mental thought about it, you know, in my head, and I can just definitely see it."

We all laugh.

"Exactly", Mo says, "The second reason why they are so attractive is, the way they jiggle; it is non-stop. Everywhere a lady wearing goes, it jiggles, she moves, it moves, and that kind of thing just automatically draws attention, you know? So, in short, that's why Nigerian men go crazy over waist beads."

We all laugh again. Just then, Mo sights another troop of new customers walk into the shop.

"Okay, guys, I have to go attend to some other customers. Just keep on browsing, and anything you want me to tell you the story off, just let me know. I like nothing more than sharing stories of my culture, except sell pieces of it, that is", Mo says, laughing.

We laugh too, and wave her on.

We turn back to perusing, and we come across a lot of cool stuff, in-depth traditional pieces, and something that looks a lot like dirt, but I'm sure it's probably not just dirt. It must be important dirt. I and Cade are bent over, looking through a glass shelf, at a live tarantula (I have never seen one before, so this is exciting for me), or it was, just before we hear a voice from behind us call out, "Cade!"

Before turning, I close my eyes, because I know that voice, I recognize that voice, loud and clear.

"Hello Natalie", Cade says, voicing out my worst fear.

MEAN GIRLS

I open my eyes, and slowly turn to face Natalie and Elena, the two people I really don't want to see. But society demands courtesy, so I smile, and I can feel it's fake, because my face hurts from doing it, but I don't care. Society can suck it. I fake-smile, "Elena, Natalie", I say, nodding slightly.

Natalie's eyes start, very slowly- and I'm sure, deliberately- from my face, down to my chest, my legs, my boot-clad feet. She brings it back to my face, her face bored. While she was having her classic mean girl moment, Cade and Elena had been quiet, both staring between the two of us. Now, as Natalie brings her eyes back to my face, and still says nothing, just stares at me with a bored expression.... Elena breaks the silence with a forceful laugh.

"Hi, Olivia! Fancy meeting you here!", more forceful laughter, "I mean, what are the odds of us meeting here, a tourist shop, that's not too far from either of the places we're each lodging."

At this, we all slowly turn to look at Elena, she realizes what she just said, her face freezes, and then, "Hahaha", more forceful laughter.

Cade clears his throat, Natalie gives Elena a scathing look, and then turns to Cade, her face impressively transforming. Her whole face lights up, "Hi, Cade", she says, her voice saccharine sweet.

I roll my eyes.

Cade just nods, his face impassive, beside him, I can feel his rigidness coming off of him in waves.

Natalie's eyes narrow slightly, she definitely felt the cold. Elena gives her a nervous look, and chuckles; Elena clearly doesn't work well under pressure.

"So, what are you guys doing here?", she asks.

"Shopping", Cade replies shortly, leaving it at that.

Silence descends again, and Elena wrings her hands together, fraught. Natalie doesn't say anything, she just stares at Cade, blatantly ignoring my presence.

Sucks for you, I think to myself, a person can't be erased from existence by sheer thoughts of another. Trust me, if that were possible, this situation wouldn't be happening right now. The silence stretches, and I see Elena biting on her lower lip, the distress clearly on her face. From the little time we spent together, I know out of the two ladies, Elena was the vibrant one, she loved life, and it was clear from the way she lived it so freely. I don't actually have anything against Elena, sure she could be too much at times, but a vibrant person like Elena couldn't be less, even if she tried.

I decide to help her out, "We're browsing. Mo, the owner of the shop, is a Nigerian, and most of the items here are Nigerian traditional items, relating to their culture. We think it's fascinating", I say, smiling up at Cade.

He smiles back, looking down at me, and just like that, we can't seem to stop smiling at each other. I guess Elena and Natalie were staring at us as we grinned like fools at each other, because after a moment, Natalie clears her throat. We break up our smile bubble, and turn to look at her. She serves me an icy cold look, before turning to Cade, again, with the magical transformation of face. "Cade, so, we never did finish out talk, back at the bonfire. Think we could get together sometime? Talk?", she eyes me, and adds, "Alone."

Wow, this bitch's got levels.

Cade's hand comes around my shoulders, he gently, but very clearly, tucks me against his side. I watch Elena and Natalie's eyes follow the action, Elena's eyebrows go up, her eyes widening a little bit, on the other hand, Natalie's eyes narrow, and I can tell she doesn't like what she's seeing.

"Actually, no, that won't be possible. Olivia and I made it official, I'm hers, we're each other's, and I don't think she'd appreciate me going on a date with you. Right, babe?"

Elena's eyes are now like huge round saucers, her mouth agape, Natalie grits her teeth together, and they are so tight I can almost feel the pain of it from where I'm standing. But I don't even process their reactions well, because Cade's words are still ringing in my head, 'I'm hers, we're each other's', wow.

I look up at him, and find him already looking down at me, his expression tender. Mine soften, and I can feel my heart in my chest growing, but not growing tight, no, this time, it's more like my heart is expanding with joy.

I smile, and still looking at Cade, I reply, "No, I wouldn't like that", Cade grins, and his handsome face lights up. I look at Natalie, and I make sure she is looking right back at me, I stare her dead in the eye, and complete my earlier statement, "I don't like to share."

Her eyes narrow again, and I have to admit, she does have that intimidating look down pat, and in any other situation, on any other day, I probably would have felt intimidated by it, but not today. No, today is different, today I feel like I can hang the moon, so I stare right back at her. I don't try the intimidating angle; that's Natalie's style, instead I just hold my own against her; that's my style. We stare at each other like this for a full minute, nobody talks, and then Natalie breaks the contact. She gives me an evil look, which I just smirk to; you lose, sucker.

She turns to Cade, but just as she's about to talk, he cuts her off, "We are not done browsing, so we'll be on our way now, you guys have fun", he takes my hand, gives Natalie a cool nod, and smiles a little at Elena, and tugs me away.

We walk away, and towards a shelf a few feet away from them. Cade turns to me, "Are you okay?", he asks.

"Oh, yeah, I'm fine." Cade's eyes narrow like he doesn't believe me. "I swear I'm fine, really", I say, chuckling.

He looks at me for a minute longer, and then he backs down, "Okay."

"It takes more than a few bitchy words to get to me, you know?", I say.

Cade sighs, "I know, I know. I just, God, she's a handful", he says, shaking his head a little.

My lips twitch, "Looks like I should be the one asking you if you're okay", I tease him.

He laughs, "Maybe. It will forever be beyond me why some people are like that; manipulative and just plain bad. I mean, why be bad, when you can just be good? Like, it's that's simple", Cade says.

I shrug, "Yeah, well, people like Natalie don't see it that way. Most of the time, people like her need to be hurtful to other people, they find it very hard to feel good about themselves unless somebody else feels bad about themselves, so they set out to do the deed", I shrug again, "Bullies like that should be pitied, really. I mean, I pity her. Because when it all comes down to it, when you really think about it, it's a lot of work to be bad, it must be really stressful, finding the negative in every situation, being sour when everyone else is happy, and so on like that."

"Wow, now I do feel bad for her", Cade says, looking at me with something like pride in his eyes, and then he out rightly says the word, "I am proud of you."

"Why?", I ask, truly confused.

"Well, you know, just seeing the situation in that kind of way, a way that is not what it looks like, at all", Cade says, "That takes gut."

A new type of feeling washes over me, and I realize I like the feeling of Cade being proud of me.

We browse for a little while longer, Natalie and Elena are long gone now, Mo walks towards us.

"So, you guys need anything? Anything catch your fancy?", Mo asks, smiling warmly at us.

Cade lifts up a native top with short sleeves, with painted art inscriptions on them, in bright colors, "What is this?", he asks.

"That is called a Dashiki, it is generally men's wear, a traditional outfit that is usually worn to special occasions and celebrations, but now, some women wear it too", Mo explains.

Cade puts the outfit to his chest, looking down at the way it looks on him.

"That would look really good on you, your complexion is a really flattering one", Mo says.

"Thank you. You know, I think I'll take it, I really like it", Cade says.

"Nice. What about you, Olivia?", Mo turns to me.

Cade turns to me too, and they both look at me expectantly. I shift on my feet nervously, "You go ahead, I will just browse a little more", I say, praying Cade doesn't push it. But of course, he does, he looks at me, "Hey, you okay?", he asks.

I shrug, "Yeah, yeah, I'm fine. Just go on, I'll be right with you in a minute", I say, subtly pushing him away.

He gives me a weird look, but he allows himself to be pushed, "Okay, I'll be at checkout then", he says.

I nod, "Okay."

He starts to go, and then he turns to me again, "You're sure you're good, right?", he asks again.

I laugh, and this time, I push him not so subtly, "I said I'm fine, really. Go."

Finally, he leaves, following Mo to the checkout counter. Once they're out of sight, I turn back, and head towards the shelf we first stopped at when we came in. I look at the waist beads Mo explained to us earlier, I smile to myself; is Cade in for a treat!

I am still looking at the beads, when I hear a voice behind me, "You think you're all that now, don't you?"

I turn to find Natalie looking at me with one of her iciest looks ever, her lackey is nowhere to be found. I give her a bored look, because that's all the effort I'm giving her, I even sigh, before I ask, "What do you want, Natalie?"

Natalie is an impressive five feet, so when she walks closer to me, and puts her face directly in front of mine, I have to tilt my head back a little to meet her gaze. I bet she knows just how powerful her height and body build are, and she milks them for all they are worth, she looks at me dead in my eyes, her icy look frosting over. "You think you're all that, nina?", she says the 'nina' with a sneer, and somehow that pisses me off more than anything else, but she continues before I can say anything, "You think because Cade is looking at you like he's doing, he likes you?"

When she doesn't say anything else, and just looks at me, I move my eyeballs like, "Yeah, I think that's exactly what it means."

I can almost see the steam coming out of her ears as she realizes I'm not in the least bit fazed by her words. "You listen to me, Cinderella, Cade is not going to be interested in you for much longer. Girls like you don't have the power to hold a guy's attention for long, talk less of Cade", she takes a step further to me, putting more steel in my voice, "Cade is a man, a strong virile man, believe me, in the little time we spent together, I noticed. You think you know what a guy like him wants? You don't. And you never will. But me? Oh, I know all about what a guy like Cade wants, I know what he needs, and I am ready to give it to him, six ways to Sunday." She leans back, a smirk on her face, clearly celebrating her delivery of shade.

I just smile, the words I said to Cade earlier on about Natalie, coming back to me. I look at her, her impressive huge build, her busty breasts almost popping out of the snug top she wore, her excessive makeup that makes her look more like a cheap drag queen, than a human being, and the hate in her eyes, a hate that is only masking a more vulnerable emotion; fear, and all I feel is pity for her.

I don't get in her face like she did me, I remain standing where I am, the words I'm about to say will deliver loud and clear, and just fine from where I'm standing. "You said it all, Natalie, 'from the little time you spent with him', that's all you are ever going to have with him; a little time. We have been on the road together for almost a week now, and now, we are together again, I don't need to try so hard, or stalk him to a tourist shop", I watch her eyes narrow as I say this, *nailed it,* I hadn't even known that to be true, per se, I was just spit balling, but seems like I hit the nail right on the head. "I don't need to be that desperate, because I am not you, Natalie, and I never want to be. And you do know there is life outside a bedroom, right? You could know everything there is to know about pleasing a man in the bedroom, but you are going to have to come out of there eventually, and then what, Natalie? Then what?" I pause, letting that sink in. Natalie's eyes narrow to stilts, she grits her teeth, clearly angry, maybe at me, maybe at herself, maybe at both, that is yet to be known, but she is angry.

Somehow though, I don't know how I see it, but past her anger, and I see her fear, I see her hands tremble a little, her lower lip too.

I sigh, "Look, I don't know when you decided you had to be mean to me, maybe after the bonfire, when you wanted Cade to stay with you, but he declined, and we went to a different hotel. Maybe that made you mad, and you felt like I had something to do with it…. I didn't. I am not in a competition with you, you should stop being in an imaginary one with me. I am not your enemy, neither are you one to yourself. Love yourself, try that, and maybe then you wouldn't have to beg a man like Cade to be with you. Because if there's one thing I have learnt about Cade, and if you're willing to take my advice, is that, men like him are attracted to women who respects themselves, respect yourself first, and he'll automatically respect you." Out of the corner of my eye, I see Elena walking frantically towards us, I say my parting sentence, "I really liked you guys when we first met, really, I did, and I think you liked me too", I see the flicker of truth in Natalie's eyes, I nod, "You did. So, it would be a shame to lose what could be friendship over something so trivial as liking the same boy."

I give a small smile, I turn to take the waist bead off the shelf, Elena is now beside Natalie, I nod at them, and leave, walking towards the checkout counter, and Cade.

FIREWORKS

After a vigorous day at Venice Beach; shopping at Mo's shop, crossing paths with Elena and Natalie, not once, but twice, at least for me, and giving such an emotional speech to Natalie, Cade had asked me what took me so long, and he had tried to pry it out of me when I wouldn't say anything, but I had stood firm, and told him it was nothing. Because, in a way, for me, it really was nothing. I had said my piece to Natalie, and I had a feeling she really heard me, so there's just no point drawing it out any longer. And, it turned out putting a mean girl in her place takes a lot out of a person, so after leaving Mo's shop with our purchases, me once again hiding something from Cade; what I bought, we had gone to a restaurant, ate till we were full, and decided to do just one more round of Venice Beach before heading home. We had visited a photobooth, taking a bunch of crazy pictures, and some not so playful ones, my cheeks are heating up just thinking about them right now. After that, we had ridden on a Ferris wheel, and we had laughed so hard at each other's expenses, so much so that even now, my jaw hurts from laughing so much.

Today has been the best day I can remember ever having in a long time, and now, I'm in my hotel room, Cade's in his, and I don't know where it's coming from, but I'm feeling an odd sense of excitement. My fingertips itch, and I can't seem to stop tapping my feet on the floor. A knock sounds on my door, my tapping stops.

"Olivia?"

Cade. His name drops like a whisper from my lips. I rush to the door, and throw it open, I see him standing on the other side, his eyes saying something to me, something intimate.

"Olivia"

That's all. That's all he says, and I pull him inside, and close the door. We stand in the middle of the room, the two of us, staring at each other, and I finally know where the thrum of excitement is coming from, I can feel it coming off of him in waves too.

This is it. This is the moment of truth, and feelings. Mostly feelings. All I can do is feel, I feel the air around us charge, it is not like the other times, no, this is more. I have never felt an onslaught of feelings like this in my entire life. Cade walks toward me, slowly, or at least it seems that way to me, maybe I am just seeing things in slow motion. I feel frissons of excited electricity sneak up my arms, from the base of my fingertips, through my nerves, up my arms, and straight to my head, God, I feel the lightness, my heart starts beating fast, and I vaguely have this thought that I would pass out from anticipation before we even begin.

The orange-red light from the hotel room bedside lamp reflects in Cade's eyes, the grey in them keep the reflection isolated, so it dances lightly as his gaze remains fixated on me. I don't know when he got to my front, but suddenly, he is standing right in front of me. He places both hands on either side of my arms, and does a subtle light caress; up, down, up, down.

"You are so beautiful", he says, in a deep, gravelly voice. His words wash over me, the quietness of it made all the more intimate in the dimly lit private room. His hand comes up to my lips, and slowly, and so seductively, he runs it lightly over my lips. "You have no idea how much I have thought of this, of this moment, right here. How your lips would feel. I knew they had to be as soft as they looked, and knowing that", he chuckles shortly, and even though the action was anything but painful, I could feel his struggle, "God, knowing that, Olivia, it damn near almost killed me. But all I could do was guess, imagine. But no amount of guessing or imagining would ever give me a clue as to what you would taste like. No, it would never. Knowing that in itself was a torture too, all on its own, but it was also a reward. It gave me something to look forward to. The mystery of how you would taste, it was a reward I was glad to wait for."

While he talked, his eyes had been on my lips, tracing the movement of his fingers, now, they come up to meet mine, and the intensity in them almost has me staggering. I am sure if he isn't holding my face, serving as kind of anchor that I desperately tie myself to, I would melt into a puddle at his feet.

"I want to taste you."

He drops the words like a bomb, landing between us. He doesn't make a move though, he continues looking into my eyes, and I know he is silently asking for my permission. It would be so easy to fall into the category of one of those women that does nothing during lovemaking, that just stand there, feel, and let the man do all the stimulations, it would be so easy, because feelings assail me right now. But I have to convey all these feelings I am feeling currently, to Cade. I want to convey them, I need to. So, I frame his face in my hands, and slowly, I bring my face closer to his. When my lips are juts a whisper from his, I say, "Take it." I close my eyes, and close the distance between our lips.

To say I put my total focus into the kiss would be a gross understatement, someone could have yelled 'fire', and I would not have heard. Like Taylor Swift, a message is all I have, except for me, it is in the kiss, not a bottle. I have a message to pass across to Cade, so the kiss is more than just a kiss, it is a confession. A confession of how it wasn't only him who had thought about this moment, here and now, a confession of how I had through of it also, dreamed of it; how his lips would taste, what feelings they would evoke in me. A confession of how none of what I had ever dreamed up, comes close. Not even a little bit.

While I had always dreamed that when Cade finally kisses me, I would feel a slow burn in the pit of my stomach, now, my whole body is on fire. While I had always imagined that I probably wouldn't be able to think of anything in the moment, now, all I can think is; more. While I had always dreamed Cade's kiss would rock my world, now, I feel the earth shifting beneath my feet. We break apart, our foreheads resting on each other's, we are both panting softly. I definitely never dreamed this.

"That was-", Cade cuts off.

My forehead still on Cade's, I nod, "Yes, it was."

Cade leans back, and a little thrill runs through me when I see the intense look still in his eyes, burning bright as ever.

"I want to make you feel a lot more. I want to make love to you", Cade says, in that low gravelly voice again.

This time, he knows he doesn't have to ask for my permission. He slowly starts to peel off my top, I keep my eyes on him, his eyes trail over my body just as slowly as his hands move. "Beautiful", he whispers. Goosebumps rise over my arms, my top falls to the ground, my breasts are bare, only clad in my more-show-than-hide bra. "You are perfect", Cade says, making it sound almost like a prayer. Still taking his time, he slowly draws the hands of my bra down. Clearly, he is trying to make me go crazy, and it is working.

He leans in, and kisses me again, he means to drip a light kiss, but I take the control out of his hands for a minute, and prolong it. Our lips separate, and I give him a sultry smile as I see how it destabilizes him. He grins, and draws my bar off all the way, my breasts are now completely bare to him. He stares at them for a moment, I can't see his expression as his head is bent towards them. And then he bends over, leaning in to take one of them into his mouth. I close my eyes, and throw my head back at the sensation of his wet hot lips on my naked breasts. He plays with it for a while, nipping it with his teeth with enough force to send a thrill up my legs, and not too much that is painful. I hold his head, the pleasure slamming into me, making me arch into his mouth even more.

"Wow, you are really good at that", I ground out.

He looks up from my breasts, and something he sees on my face makes him grin, probably my flushed cheeks. "Thanks."

"You're welcome", I manage, already feeling another onslaught of pleasure building up as he rubs the peak of the other un-assaulted breast, between his thumb and forefinger. I moan quietly.

Suddenly he looks up, and now with the desire, I see another emotion burning in his eyes; possessiveness. A rush of heat fills me. Cade cups both breasts in his hands, his eyes locked on mine. "You are made for me", he says, he squeezes them a little tighter, "Me."

I nod my head, because I totally agree, nothing had ever felt more right. His hands move down my body, hugging my waist, it slips further down, to my jeans. He starts to unzip them, but I put a hand on his, halting his movement.

"You are way too dressed", I say. And then I proceed to run my hands over his arms, I feel his muscles, and muscles, firm and strong under my hands. Slowly, like he did to me, I draw up his top, Cade raises his arms above his head for me to pull them off. I fling the top, not caring where it lands, my eyes fixate on his chest, I run my hand over them again, this time feeling the warmth of his bare skin beneath my fingers. I look up into his eyes, and I make sure I lock unto them, I do not release him from my gaze as I let my hand travel further down, slowly, till it reaches the waistband of his jeans. Where his eyes had been teasing before, enjoying my exploration and curious as to how far I was going to go, they grow hot, and I can feel the heat of them on my skin, as I trace my fingers over the ridge slightly bulging through his jeans, behind his zipper.

My lips curl sultrily, I caress his arousal some more, and I feel a surge of pure feminine pride as I hear his breath hitch. His hand shoots out, and lands on mine, halting my movements.

"You don't want to be doing that, Olivia, or this could be over before it even begins", Cade grounds out through gritted teeth, the veins in his neck popping as he strains to keep it in his pants, literally.

"We do not want that", I say, enjoying myself so much.

"No, we do not", Cade replies. He frames my face, "God, you are beautiful", he says, staring at me with so much…. love? …. in his eyes.

My breath catches, I am about to reply when a strange expression washes over Cade's face. "What's wrong?", I ask.

"Please tell me you have a condom on you", Cade says, he whispers it like a prayer.

"Oh God", I say, realizing the conundrum, "Oh God", I say again.

Cade runs a hand through his hair, and closes his eyes. This cannot be happening. I can still feel the heat thrumming between us, the air is still charged, my body is still tingling. No, this cannot be happening.

And then, like a call from heaven, I remember; my wish for the day. Cade is starting to take a step back from me, I latch on to his arm, and draw him back. I draw him close to me, and rest my forehead on his, like we did before. No way this is not happening tonight, I would die before I let this beautiful, wonderful thing go, because of a lack of condom.

"Olivia", Cade says, his voice is strained, like he is trying to be strong, but I am not making it easy for him.

Oh, I love you, Cade Vulcan.

The thought washes over me quietly, and I receive it with a calmness that I do not know where it comes from. I love him. A realization that just makes my next decision a much easier one. I close my eyes, and clear my mind till all that's left is Cade, my burning desire for him, and the one thing that was stopping me from giving myself to the man I love.

"Olivia", Cade says again.

"Shh", I whisper.

I don't know how I know it, I just do, I reach into Cade's back pocket of his jeans, and pull out a condom packet.

Cade's brows furrows when he sees what I brought out. "How did that.... where did…"

"Shh", I say again, putting a finger on his lips to stop him. I hold his face in my hands, and look into his eyes, I can already feel our bodies warming up again. I have long since stopped asking myself how I could possibly feel this much for a person, I am made for Cade, he is made for me. Sometimes, it is just that simple.

"I want you", I say quietly, letting all my desire for him shine through my eyes. Cade leans in to me, and lay his lips on mine, and this time too, I just know.

I just know I am about to enter a world I have never been to before.

AFTERMATH

And he took me there, over and over again. Now, we are on the bed, snuggled up together, we just finished another round of lovemaking, this time, I had worn the waist bead I purchased from Mo. And it had been all worth it to see his Cade's eyes heat up when he saw the beads, he had been really surprised that I had bought it, and really glad that I did. The round of lovemaking had been intense, and I can still feel tingles in my body as I remember the way he had touched me, right where the beads had been resting, on my waist, in between my legs, and round my hips.

"Hmm, God bless Nigeria", Cade murmurs into my ear, tucking me more firmly under his chin.

I laugh, which comes out more like a giggle, I cannot believe how happy I am at this moment. Is this what it feels like to be in love? If it is, how could I have gone so ling without it all my life? This right here, this feeling of utter contentment, and thorough loving, that I am feeling right now in Cade's arms, this must be what life's all about. Nothing else, just this.

Cade's hands stroke my arm, up and down, in slow movements. "Man, I cannot imagine what it would have been like if I hadn't met you. I mean, can you imagine if your car hadn't broken down on the road that day, and I never showed up? We would never have had this; we would never have felt this."

As he talks, Cade slowly starts kissing my neck, trailing kisses down my arm, he looks up at me, a wide grin in his face. "Right now, I bet you love knowing me", he says, grinning, and looking like a child. Except what he is now doing to the insides of my thigh is anything but childlike.

I gasp softly as the feeling that is now familiar, starts building up inside me, again. He eats me out, and brings me to orgasm again.

"That's seven to five now, baby, breaking my own record of this night here", he says, a smug smile on his face as he pulls me close again.

"You are not counting!", I exclaim, turning to face him, a delighted surprise on my face.

"Of course, I'm counting. This is hard work, baby, hard man's work", Cade says.

I laugh, "I bet you're pretty proud of yourself right now, aren't you?", I ask, now kneeling on the bed, facing him.

His face is so relaxed, and even though I am the one who has orgasmed seven times, two more than he has, he looks like he is pretty satisfied. A silly smile is on his face, "Oh, I am", he says, in reply to my earlier statement.

He tickles me on my waist, and I fall down back on the bed, laughing so hard. We laugh like loon for a while before we finally calm down. I snuggle back in his arms, and Cade's arms come around me, holding me in tight. He doesn't say the words, but I can hear them in my head, *I love you*. Maybe it's my thoughts being so loud, maybe it's the feeling coming off of Cade and translating to the words, I don't know what it is, but I feel the words so deeply in this moment.

I close my eyes. I never want this feeling to go away, ever. But I'm afraid it just might, when Cade learns about Clive- because now I have to tell him- will it change the way he feels about me? Will I have to let him go? Let this feeling go? Suddenly, I am filled with dread.

If you liked this book

Find our fiction below!

https://www.ttpublishinghouse.com/legendsreborn

https://www.ttpublishinghouse.com/7wishes

https://www.ttpublishinghouse.com/mallcadet

Social Media

Facebook: tlmpublishinghouse

Website: www.TTpublishinghouse.com